A Sleepy

BY ELISABETH BURROWES
ILLUSTRATED BY RICHARD BROWN

A GOLDEN BOOK · NEW YORK
Western Publishing Company, Inc., Racine, Wisconsin 53404

S T

Once there was a little girl. It was time to go to sleep, but she was not sleepy. Well, maybe she was just a tiny bit sleepy.

She hopped into bed and covered
herself up to her chin with her big red blanket.
She said to her mother, "Tell me a story."

So her mother said:

Once upon a time there was a giraffe, a little giraffe with a long, long neck. It was time to go to sleep, but he was not sleepy. Well, maybe he was a tiny bit sleepy.

He said to his mother, "Tell me a story."

So his mother said:

Once upon a time there was a fox, a little red fox with a big, bushy tail. It was time to go to sleep, and he was beginning to be very sleepy.

He said to his mother, "Tell me a story."

So his mother said:

Once upon a time there was an elephant, a little gray elephant with a big, big trunk. It was time to go to sleep, and she was beginning to be just a little bit sleepy.

She said to her mother, "Tell me a story."

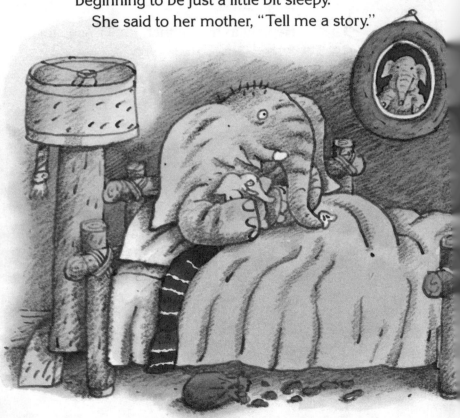

So her mother said:

Once upon a time there was a puppy,
a fluffy black puppy with floppy ears.
It was time to go to sleep, and she was
a sleepy puppy.

She said to her mother, "Tell me a story."

So her mother said:

Once upon a time there was a field mouse, a little gray field mouse with a long, skinny tail. She was a very sleepy little mouse.

She said to her mother, "Tell me a story."

So her mother said:

Once upon a time there was a pony,
a little brown pony with a thick black mane.
He was a sleepy, sleepy little pony.

He yawned. Then he said to his mother,
"Tell…me…a…story."

So his mother said:
Once upon a time…
But the little brown pony did not hear.
He was fast asleep.

So was the little gray field mouse
with the long, skinny tail.

So was the fluffy black puppy
with the floppy ears.

So was the little red fox
with the big, bushy tail.

So was the little gray elephant
with the big, big trunk.

So was the little giraffe
with the long, long neck.

And so was the little girl,
all cuddled up under her big red blanket.
All fast asleep.
Good night!